Lincolnshire Tales

Edited By Lottie Boreham

First published in Great Britain in 2017 by:

 Young**Writers** Est. 1991

Coltsfoot Drive
Peterborough
PE2 9BF
Telephone: 01733 890066
Website: www.youngwriters.co.uk

FOREWORD

Young Writers is proud to present, 'Welcome to Wonderland –
Lincolnshire Tales'.

For our latest mini saga competition, we asked secondary school
pupils to create their own Wonderland or fantasy world and
incorporate it into a story with a beginning, middle and end. On
top of this, they had the added challenge of keeping their sagas to
just 100 words!

They have risen to the challenge brilliantly and the result is this
fantastic collection of fiction, encouraging readers to explore the
creative masterpieces of our young writers. Get ready for an out-
of-this-world adventure as you discover a wealth of new worlds,
and some that are just a little bit familiar!

There was a great response to this competition which is always
nice to see, and the standard of entries was excellent, so I'd like to
say a big thank you and well done to everyone who entered.
I hope you enjoy reading these mini sagas as much as I did.

Lottie Boreham

CONTENTS

Somercotes Academy, Louth

Brandon Booth (11)	68
Daniel Straw (12)	69
Chloe Taylor (12)	70
George Thornton (11)	71
Olly Edwards (12)	72
Harry Betterridge (12)	73
William Howard	74
Charlotte Cooper (11)	75
Sam Greenwood (12)	76
Jennifer Atwell (11)	77
Isabel Wyer (12)	78
Kyle Sharp (13)	79
Oliver Toothill (12)	80
Elisé-Anais Critchley (12)	81
Charlotte Merry (12)	82
Megan Louise Whetstone (13)	83
Chloe Motson (12)	84
Liljan Tindalid (11)	85
Katie Swallow (12)	86
Idena Short (11)	87
Claudia Senior (13)	88
Liam Wright (11)	89
Emily Ackroyd (12)	90
Onyx Clancy (11)	91
Reece Cook (11)	92
Manisha Bains (13)	93
Hope Midgley (13)	94
Isobel Russell (12)	95
Evie Dinah Ann Kidd (12)	96
Lydia Wright (13)	97
Ella Pickard (11)	98
Isabell Harris (13)	99
Aaron Steer (12)	100
Thea Hussey (11)	101
Jessica Butterfield (12)	102
Leah Hezzell	103
Ellie Rusling (12)	104
Billie Jay Wilson (13)	105
Eliot James Coleman (11)	106
Charlotte Wright (11)	107
Lucy-Leigh Killick	108
Oscar Wilson (11)	109

Skie Jasmine Shelton (12)	110
Charlie Beevers (12)	111
Leo Burch (12)	112
Grace Power (11)	113
Travis Broughton (11)	114
James Garcia-Fussey (12)	115
Teanna Willey (11)	116
Rebecca Jeffrey (12)	117
Maisie Thomas (12)	118
Benjamin Thomas Jackson (12)	119
Daisy Tellefsen (11)	120
Harriet Gilliatt (11)	121
Freya Elise Donner (13)	122
Ryan Tomlinson (11)	123
Kristian Sivertsen (12)	124
Leo Jacob Whittaker (11)	125
George Crawford (12)	126
Jake Mudie (13)	127
Hollie-Mae Smith (12)	128
Amy Baxter-Rowson (11)	129
Jack Row (11)	130
Frazer Perrow (11)	131
Joe Bradley Jordan (11)	132
Oliver Greenway (11)	133
Tarn Nicholls (12)	134
Alysia Lloyd-Clews (12)	135

Spalding Academy, Spalding

Ruby Grace Allen (11)	136
Georgiana Comanescu (13)	137
Ketia Ela Lace (13)	138
Brayden Hagon (12)	139
Deborah Batch (14)	140
Emma Clark (13)	141
Erin Langford (11)	142
Hannah Dawson (14)	143
Connor Young (14)	144
Millie Bailey (11)	145
Jantraskin Jan (14)	146
Tyler James Boon (11)	147
Maria Chirita (11)	148
Grace Woods (15)	149
Caitlin Langford (14)	150

THE MINI SAGAS

Where We Belong...

Walking home one day, sunny and bright, I was sucked into a strong wind, which was a multi-coloured tornado. I don't know what happened, but I do know that later I was lying on a vast cushion. Suddenly, an odd figure advanced. Scared, I ran! I stopped when I heard the creature say, 'Me, help, please, I've not had such easy ride as you, I lost legs that replaced with kangaroo!'

I sighted a lion with kangaroo legs. I helped him.

Together, we went to find the same tornado so it could take us back to where we belonged…

Kishna Haldipur (11)
Queen Elizabeth's High School, Gainsborough

Promises

'Come on quick,' whispered Josh. 'Hurry up.'

'Josh, he would have k-killed me if you hadn't... ' Mark stuttered.

He looked across the calm water and sat on the cold bank.

'How could this happen?' Josh asked. 'There hasn't been a murder in years, it's a small town, people don't die here!' he exclaimed.

'He just killed them,' Mark mumbled, his voice weak.

'We can't tell anyone, if they found out what we were doing here my dad would kill me,' Josh panicked.

'Okay,' Mark sighed. He leant over and kissed him. 'I promise I won't tell anyone who you are!'

Emily Scott (13)
Queen Elizabeth's High School, Gainsborough

The Murderer

A young man entered through the weathered door. A silhouette appeared across the dampened wall and an authoritative voice boomed, 'What are you doing back here?'
The boy responded, 'I'm here to ensure your safety as I heard a murderer had escaped in the local vicinity.' The gust whistled in the background and the inferno in the fireplace danced erratically. From the corner of the young man's eye he glimpsed a gleaming blade, but did not comprehend the situation.
Abruptly trepidation spread his face, which the older man observed. He eviscerated repeatedly and murmured, 'No one may know my secret, son!'

Harvey Shek (13)
Queen Elizabeth's High School, Gainsborough

Catastrophe

The cat planet, a place of peace and kindness. But this was about to change.

Two cats looked back at their planet. They could see lots of fragments of planet. 'How many kittens survived?' whispered Tiddles.

'I don't know,' replied Felix. They landed on the remains of their planet. It was as though time stood still. The only movement was a little orange flame.

The landscape was dotted with small remains of civilisations living in enclosed spaces which weren't destroyed by the impact. 'Why are there fragments?' Tiddles asked.

'Because the impact threw bits of our planet away!' he replied.

Jacob Holmes (11)
Queen Elizabeth's High School, Gainsborough

October 28th 1962

The sirens rang. It was time. A year in hiding. Had anyone made it? The solid metal door opened.

Outside the wind whistled through the desolate street, wearing around the abandoned skyscrapers. *Clack, clack.* The heels of the President's shoes pounded the radiated tarmac. 'So this is what's left? It didn't have to come to this. It didn't have to be like this. All of this from one phone call. He didn't have to threaten them, his brilliant idea backfired on him.'

'Nuclear missiles,' they said, 'enough to hold them back,' they said. 'No one was prepared for what happened!'

Shabab Rahman (13)
Queen Elizabeth's High School, Gainsborough

Shadow Silhouette...

The midnight sky glistened in the moonlight whilst a blanket of mist fell from above. I squinted, the grass parted swiftly as the wind raced through the rustling trees. An echo, a crunch nearby from the gloomy bed of trees. My heart in my jaw-dropped mouth thudded repeatedly, hands-trembling and traumatised. I peered carefully towards the sea of leaves and branches. A glimmer met my eye, a glimmer of hope or doom! Heart-pulsing, blood gushing through the veins beneath my ghostly pale skin, my bleeding ears were triggered... A crunching noise followed from my silhouette. Swiftly, I stumbled upon... 'Argh!'

Harrison Andrew Place (11)
Queen Elizabeth's High School, Gainsborough

The Invasion

Mess everywhere! Smashed vehicles and other objects had been thrown onto the streets as though they weren't wanted. They didn't care. They had everything from handy hovercrafts to floating robots. We had to sit there, powerless against the horror before us. They made us sit there and watch them demolish our homes and everything inside them. Children that hated going to school cried whilst watching the school being destroyed. There were smashed windows and broken doors. Everyone was devastated. No one knew what was going to happen. Where would we live? What would happen now the aliens had invaded?

Ella Letorey (12)
Queen Elizabeth's High School, Gainsborough

I'm Happy, I Know It

I'm happy you know? I thought, looking at the towering glistening buildings. Looking around all I saw were robots. Same jacket. Same tie. Same trousers.
Neon yellow and pink flowers with their stiff stems not even waving in the wind of the hovercrafts. I strode back to my dingy apartment. It wasn't as luxurious as the robots'... But it'd do for us humans. I tossed my jacket to the sofa making a picture ricochet to the ground. I peered at the photo. 'Claire... What they did to you was unacceptable!' I yelled. 'The robots need to go... They must die...'

Lana Glendenning (13)
Queen Elizabeth's High School, Gainsborough

England 2042, It's Upon Us!

England 2042, it's upon us!

I was getting up ready for school and I knew that today was going to be amazing. Oh, I'm Casey, eleven years old and I can't wait to see my favourite celebrity. Screeching, us girls ran in, he was there, the best pop star, Alec McFauld...

Boom... Bang... The lights flickered. 'Evacuate the building now! Evacuate now! Hurry, quick!' Everyone ran outside screaming for their lives. The explosion had taken my best friend Keira. Knocked to the ground the darkness swallowed me up. Goodbye world.

World War Three had started! England 2042, it's upon us!

Casey King (11)
Queen Elizabeth's High School, Gainsborough

Break Free

My new school was stunning, nothing like anything in America. 'Hi you must be Lola? I'm Chad.' No one told me there were angels at this school!

'I'm supposed to be North Wing, but I got lost,' I replied.

'Don't worry, we all did, follow me,' he exclaimed. I quickly followed him.

'This is your room-mate Kelly, I'll see you later.'

Kelly then decided to take me shopping. 'So see anyone you like?' she asked. But, before I could answer, *bang!* A bullet straight through me. I gasped, awoke in a hospital bed. Was it all just a dream?

Poppy Edlington (12)
Queen Elizabeth's High School, Gainsborough

Hidden In Exile

Fifty years ago... It was finally time. Harry camped underground in his secret bunker for almost five years! As he was a fugitive, he could only come out at night. Finding supplies was proving hard.

Then one day, whilst searching for supplies, something abysmal happened, something he'd never seen before... Harry lay down on his concrete bed exhausted. He was like a nocturnal animal. Today, 1950, something strange happened. There he heard a sinister sound. He peered around the corner and stumbled upon two giant flying robots! Life then was hard. Spookily, they sensed him. They were hunting him down...

Marco Xue (11)
Queen Elizabeth's High School, Gainsborough

The Fattest Guy Ever

Lying in a gargantuan bed in a lifeless desert was an astonishingly fat guy. His belly was so immense when he blasted off to space, space scientists reported they discovered a new gas giant planet dubbed 'Planet Nine' (which was his belly). When he turned over, onto his back, and his belly towards the air, space satellites instantly detected a new mountain, fifty times the height of Mount Everest (which was his belly). The tectonic plate underneath him shattered under his monstrous weight. The fat guy fell. When he landed, he caused a catastrophic mass extinction. And an earthquake...

Ali Sultanzadeh (14)
Queen Elizabeth's High School, Gainsborough

Eternia

I can't believe what I am witnessing. The exquisite elegance of Eternia towers over my head and colossal mountains encircle me in their grasp. Futuristic vehicles, unseen in any of the cities before, leisurely slither around bends and turns. Through the glass jungles, skyscrapers flourish from the concrete metropolis beneath. Sudden confounding thoughts of this fantasy world oblige me to realise how voguish we seem compared to the world! Skies of scarlet are soon painted a dark hue of indigo, and through the arrays of cotton clouds, invades a jet. But not just any kind of jet, a warfare fighter jet!...

Musa Jadoon (12)
Queen Elizabeth's High School, Gainsborough

Etheria

'Prepare for dimensional shift in three! Two! One!' a deep voice boomed.

Suddenly the room around me turned into what looked to be a universe closing in on me at a rapid pace, my insides feeling like they were about to come out. 'Dimensional shift complete,' a robotic, female voice announced. We had arrived back into the Etherverse, an unstable dimension where none of the laws of the universe applied, and only ghouls roamed free. Humans tampering with the fabric of space had released the ghouls into our universe.

Our mission: Head to Planet Etheria and destroy the ghoul live-mind.

Zain Khan (13)

Queen Elizabeth's High School, Gainsborough

Nightmare

The trees glistened in the soft sunlight. Everything was still and silent. I waited a long moment before I spoke to the person beside me, 'Do you think there will be more, more screaming and crying, more soldiers, more planes flying overhead dropping bombs?' My best friend sighed, a sad look crossed her pale face.

'I don't know Lucy, maybe, no one can predict things like that.' Suddenly sirens started wailing. We ran. People started screaming. Babies started crying, people were falling dead, littering the floor. We ran on. I stopped. There on the floor, lying dead, was my mother.

Hannah Keeley (11)
Queen Elizabeth's High School, Gainsborough

Unusual Sky

The streets were bursting and a sheet of snow started to fall. I was wandering the city, searching for a gift, when the sky changed. Blue turned black while gushing winds drowned out hushed voices. Bright lights blinded passersby and everyone's attention engaged on the unusual sky. A huge form of transport emerged from the clouds and as I adjusted to the colours, my vision became clear. UFOs. Their sirens and lights dulled but their small act of kindness was wasted and everyone ran. It's not clear what happened after, only that I have green friends and aliens for parents...

Ella Broomfield (12)
Queen Elizabeth's High School, Gainsborough

You Love This Place

A rat scuttled around at her feet, its sharp claws scraped the cobblestone. Its tail dragged through a puddle and the water rippled outwards. Ethne looked up to the foggy sky. A drop of rain landed on her forehead and trickled down her nose. A slender shadow cast on the perishing grey walls, looming over Ethne. More rain proceeded to fall down her face onto the cobbled floors. Except it wasn't rain, it was tears. Little salty drops of pain generated from Ethne's eyes. *It's beautiful isn't it Ethne? The adorable little rats and grey skies. You love this place...*

Lucy Mason-Watson (12)
Queen Elizabeth's High School, Gainsborough

Food Fight

Stood in the factory, I studied the situation. Food was splattered around on the marble floor. People lay stuck in sauce and slushies; it was New Year!
I ran and picked up a frying pan, using it to catapult eggs and cover the winter-white walls with stains. Someone sprinted to see what was happening, but got battered (literally). There was only a few people left to beat. Suddenly, the glass roof smashed and the nuclear sandwich producer blew up. Instinctively I ran for cover, but found myself circled. I wouldn't be promoted for winning the impossibly hard food fight frenzy!

Ewan Baker (11)
Queen Elizabeth's High School, Gainsborough

Dead Inside

Staggering to my feet, my vision sharpening, I found myself looking upon my ultimate creation. The lifeless corpses of those massacred in the purge littered the ground around a raging maelstrom of shadows that tore apart Cydonia. This was necessary, however. Happiness and joy were an epidemic, and as president of what was moments ago a bustling country, it fell upon my shoulders to neutralise the threat it posed. Now all that remained of the nation were deathly silent ruins, the rest of Cydonia burning in an endless inferno. Smiling, I looked upon my creation and I thought it good.

Conaer Wilson-Macpherson (13)
Queen Elizabeth's High School, Gainsborough

Ruin

Everything was completely obliterated. Little to no life left. I looked around at my four team members, Lauren, Dinah, Ally and Normani. I took a deep breath and shakily sighed as we took a step down from the helicopter. 'You OK Walls?' Dinah asked, concerned. She always knew how to annoy me even with the use of my old nickname.
'Yeah, I'm just peachy,' I replied sarcastically. I turned away and began to look through the rubble and remains. As the rest of the girls shortly followed suit, we started our much overdue search for what we so desperately needed.

Emily Roberts (14)
Queen Elizabeth's High School, Gainsborough

Betrayed

I was escorted out the car into the massive building. I could hear the rain crashing down outside and then I saw him. He sat on a large throne as I kneeled before him with my head banging down. 'Why are you here?' he asked, knowing the answer.

'I killed him,' I admitted.

'You killed who?'

'Your son, the man who betrayed me.' The room fell silent.

'How did he?' the man asked.

'I stole food because I had none, he was the only man who knew, but then he told you!' I exclaimed. 'What are we going to do?'

Freddie Moody (13)
Queen Elizabeth's High School, Gainsborough

Welcome To Wonderland

The large, oak, decrepit door towered over me. I felt like I was in a scene of a horror story. My vigorously shaking hands lifted to reach the loose handle.

Opening the door, I was expecting a deserted miserable house. However, in front of me stood a beautiful creation; above me was a clear blue sky and beneath me laid neon green grass that supported my rattling body. My confused mind spun, where was I? It was a land for the careless. A woman in a floor length dress approached me whispering, 'Welcome to Wonderland, Alice.'

Suddenly it all came back...

Emmelia Sakellariou (13)
Queen Elizabeth's High School, Gainsborough

America's Trump Card

I woke up to a sunny morning and it was the day of the American election. Possibly the worst two candidates America has ever seen.

One is obsessed with walls. Another is very bad. The election came. Jonald had won. Randomly, walls started to appear and Mexicans were vanishing into thin air. Mexican food was my favourite and I wasn't going to get any anymore. Air turned into fake tan. Bombs started to blow and the world had become terrible. Americans decided to recount the votes. Cilary had actually won. Suddenly Mexicans started to reappear and the walls got destroyed.

Jacob Bradford (11)
Queen Elizabeth's High School, Gainsborough

Midnight's Call

I stumbled through the midnight forest. Fingers scratched my pale face, bats cackled overhead. Vision distorted, I hadn't slept for days. I don't know why I crept out of bed. Entranced, my eyes hollow, I limped further and further into the night. I stopped. A chilling wail pumped fear into my body. Louder. Louder. My vision was blurring, spinning out of control. Until I saw... It. All of the rest of the world melted away as I stepped uneasily towards the wise oak that stood before me. As my blood-tingled fingers grazed its bark, I was transported far, far away...

Olivia Freeman (11)
Queen Elizabeth's High School, Gainsborough

The End

The end or the beginning depending on who wins. The Devastators or The Savers as we're called. Five people from five worlds each with inhuman abilities. One that can bend light, one that has incredible strength, another has control over the four elements, one can move at the speed of light and then there's me. The Commander. The one that's always overlooked. The archer. There are five worlds, one for all of us. Four of them obliterated, destroyed by The Devastators. The fifth where the fight begins. The fight where the world is destroyed or saved. We have to win.

Freddie Coulson (11)
Queen Elizabeth's High School, Gainsborough

Planet Nine And Three Quarters

Far away there's a planet called Planet Nine and Three Quarters. This planet is a wizardry planet (not Hocus Pocus wizardry, it's Harry Potter wizardry). Also people here are quite strange.

Anyway, I am Zack and I live on the first quarter of Planet Nine. Right now they are building the last quarter of the planet, so it will just be called Planet Ten. Here it is pretty cool with magic and... I can't really say anything else about Planet Nine. But I have always wanted to visit Earth, apparently it's amazing! But sadly I won't be visiting Earth soon!

Alice Crashley (11)
Queen Elizabeth's High School, Gainsborough

Winter Wonderland Or So It Seemed

As I stepped through the miniature door everything seemed to be beautiful and white but that did not last for long. The bombs dropped that night like it was raining, it didn't stop until the morning. Nobody knew where they were from. Dead bodies lined the streets and the catastrophe showed as the sun rose. The phone lines were down and nobody knew where everyone was. The bombs showered down for the next three nights and took the lives of many other people. *What is going on?* everyone wondered. The place that everyone thought was Heaven soon turned into Hell.

Ella Thornton (14)
Queen Elizabeth's High School, Gainsborough

No Escape

Blazing fire. Smoke polluting the air and my lungs. Sirens are wailing in the distance. I can see people's mouths moving, but no sound is reaching my ears!

The fire roars louder. I try moving. I'm too weak, like all the energy has been sucked out of me by a vacuum cleaner. Air escapes from me. I can't breathe. I collapse in exhaustion.

Not a single thought enters my head. Not one single thought.

The sunset orange and the bright yellow fire closes in on me. Will I escape? How can I?

My mind breaks free, my body remains lifeless!

Lauren Smith (12)
Queen Elizabeth's High School, Gainsborough

Journey To Glowing Eyes

The sun set in a twist of colours, disappearing from the horizon. The moon rose to the middle of the sky at twilight. I paced in the shadows of the forest towards the village. The paths were muddled and the leaves had decorated the floor in amber colours. My heavy footsteps broke the silence, yet you could still hear a pin drop. I'd been walking for ages, the paths grew to be identical. I wasn't alone! Twigs viciously snapped from behind. Boosts of adrenaline gave me strength to power through the forest maze. I turned. The glowing eyes froze. Staring!

Chantelle Sophia Mumby (14)
Queen Elizabeth's High School, Gainsborough

Wiped Out

England, 2093: nothing to do here now, all adults are wiped out. Pretty boring, although I dread to become eighteen, because I'll be wiped out! Us children try our best to make the most of our lives, we may be the last generation after all! It's scarier now, imagine having no siblings, coming home to an empty house, sleeping, eating alone, having dinner... all alone. There's nothing left in most shops due to bad children, but now they get away with everything; no adults to tell them off. If you have your mates I guess it can be bearable.

Olivia Gull (12)
Queen Elizabeth's High School, Gainsborough

A Whole New World

In the morning I rose up and looked out of my window. It was very unusual. I went straight downstairs to meet Mum and Dad, but they weren't there. So I thought I wpuld go down to meet my mates and play some football. They weren't there either! I shouted, 'Where is everybody?' Everything seemed different. I lay distraught on my bed, waiting to see anyone, then I saw something. It was an alien!

I wondered where I was until I added things together: rocky, no one was here, even smaller surroundings and aliens. I was on the planet Pluto!

Arjun Dosajh (11)
Queen Elizabeth's High School, Gainsborough

The Footballing Frenzy

Six minutes is the amount of added time, and we've already had seven. The Morati Cup, Jersey versus Guernsey, and neither team could want this more. Then, in the last second, Colin Rickshaw pounces on a through ball from Stan Mineham. He's about to take it round the keeper, Mark Altoft, when all of a sudden he sticks a leg out and trips him up. Penalty! Colin runs up to take it...

And smashes it top corner! The Jersey fans go ballistic! Colin Rickshaw, forever known as the Jersey hero! The spectacular eighteen-year-old could never have been prouder.

Arthur Altoft (12)
Queen Elizabeth's High School, Gainsborough

The Plane Crash

My eyes flickered open as I began to awaken from the vicious bang that shook me up. Trying to manoeuvre my neck, I yelled out in pain. Slowly looking around, I tried to remember what happened. Glass shattered everywhere, blood splattered everywhere, no movement; just a plane in a stranded jungle. Suddenly, I started to hear something. A small crackling sound. Then a cry of help hummed in my head. Black filled my mind as fast as lightning. Standing there, unaware of what happened, I started to worry until I realised I had to get myself together and help out.

Anell Pond (13)
Queen Elizabeth's High School, Gainsborough

The Broken Shoes

The bell of the door jingles behind me. I am going into the most miraculous shop I've seen. My first pair of pointe shoes. The silky satin lies perfectly on my feet. My first pointe class rolls around and I gently slide my feet into place.

'Stand,' says the teacher, 'now kick.' It all happened in slow motion after that. My foot slowly appearing. I see girls around me start to laugh. My toes were poking out the top. I go home in tears. Little do I know my mum has bought me the most expensive pair of pointe shoes.

Mia Fisher (12)
Queen Elizabeth's High School, Gainsborough

The Mysterious Beast

The wind woke me. I sat up shaking and gasped because of a terrible sight.

Horses sprawled on the floor. I noticed that they all looked like they had been attacked by another creature with four hooves. Hiding behind a tree were two horses that looked frightened. I shouted to comfort them; all that came out was a grunt. They replied with whimpers. As I looked behind me I saw something shaking. My body had four sharp hooves and wings, I realised why they were scared of me now. I was the four-hooved beast that had attacked all the horses.

Kate Saxby (13)
Queen Elizabeth's High School, Gainsborough

Christmas Day

The Christmas dinner was presented nicely with the hot, pleasurable turkey on the table. Turning around I saw the cold, fragile snow falling onto the even ground. Later, I went into the delightful, cosy, formal room. The Christmas tree was tall and elegant with the presents neatly organised. Leaning forward to grab a present I suddenly heard a loud noise. Turning my head upwards, the tree fell straight towards my body. Screaming loudly, the lights wrapped around me and I was stuck! Trying to get myself out of the tree, my dog ran towards me and licked my face.

Naomi Kenyon (12)
Queen Elizabeth's High School, Gainsborough

Different

The most inhuman-looking creatures I have ever seen.
Some big, some small, some dark, some not all right before
my very eyes. A whole other world I was unable to see and
now I'm standing in it, its contents spread out before me.
This path I'm standing on, this path I'm walking down is
unlike any other. It doesn't feel like my path, it's so foreign to
me, but yet it does. There is something about these
creatures, something different... I can't quite think what it is,
but then I can't really think at all. They all seem... magical.

Zoe Broomfield (13)
Queen Elizabeth's High School, Gainsborough

The Island

I looked into the distance and saw my destination. I could see people playing, having fun and running around. Mothers were watching and talking to each other. Ben jumped up in excitement and pointed over towards the island, 'Look Mummy look!' I smiled and relaxed into my seat. Ben was running in circles waiting for the boat to stop. Finally we felt it stop and he ran into the distance. I walked off the boat and saw people running around killing each other and women cheering. I turned to look for the boat, but it was nowhere to be seen.

Dominic Thomson (13)
Queen Elizabeth's High School, Gainsborough

War Zone

Bangs and booms fill the countryside followed by deafeningly loud screams. The bangs jolt me every time although you would've thought I'd be used to it by now. It helped when I had my loving family stood by me, but now they've gone, I'm all alone. Forever. Sirens ring in my head, bangs deafen me and screams scare me. Since the war started and my parents and sister passed away, all I've felt is lonely and afraid. My empty stomach is rumbling and my throat is as dry as a bone. I haven't eaten or drank in weeks, maybe months...

Lauren Vaughan (13)
Queen Elizabeth's High School, Gainsborough

The Abandoned City

'We're here Dad!' I shout, then my dad lowers me and Bob down with his chopper. It's midnight at New Year's Eve and we've decided to make a tiny visit to a spooky place on a peak of a mountain. We enter as we see a sign saying: The Abandoned City. We look around, it's all dark and cloudy with mysterious sounds also being made. Bob starts to get scared, I forgot he was frightened of the dark. There are stinking skeletons around, this place looks like an old graveyard. We get terrified and then we start running for help.

Darim Arfeen (12)
Queen Elizabeth's High School, Gainsborough

A Different World

My legs trembled as I walked through the abandoned street where bodies were littered and scattered. I could faintly hear marching and shouting from several streets away from me. As the marching got closer I started to understand what was happening. I hid in my house and peered out the window. They were after me and the others alike. As I peeked for the second time I saw them restraining an old man who was wearing an armband with the Star of David on it. They took him away with no hesitation. What if Hitler hadn't won World War Two?

Joshua Myera (13)
Queen Elizabeth's High School, Gainsborough

Dead Or Alive

Joe picked up his guitar, Jimmy took the microphone, and finally Ron sat at his drums, sticks in hand. Together they played and became the most popular musicians in the land. They travelled worldwide and spread like a virus through the web. It was their last day on tour when... disaster struck. There was a gunshot and Joe fell to the floor like a rag-doll. Everyone fled the area, except Joe, he laid there still, alone on the stage. He'd been shot, but not killed. The bullet had entered his jaw, he only played dead, to not to be dead.

Alex Mason-Watson (12)

Queen Elizabeth's High School, Gainsborough

The Chamber

Surrounded by my kind, encased by wire. We talked about our future, what awaited on the other side of those doors. Days passed, more and more of us passed through the doors, but I was still waiting. Soon there were few of us. Then one day I was picked, I'd be free. I was escorted to the doors by two armed guards with another group behind me. The doors opened. I walked down a corridor into a chamber. The doors locked. It became hard to breathe. *This is not freedom!* I thought to myself, then our bodies hit the floor.

William Taylor (13)
Queen Elizabeth's High School, Gainsborough

A Bus Ride To Hell

As the bus turned the nearest corner, I stepped out from under the battered shelter. I felt the cold rain hitting my head with force. The bus pulled up and made screeching sounds as it stopped. It looked like an ordinary bus, so I jumped on. The bus driver didn't look at me, it was as if I wasn't there. I sat down and the bus jolted forward at speed, it was a double-decker. I looked around, nobody was speaking, they were still, like mannequins, and then I realised this definitely wasn't an ordinary bus... This was a mistake!

Rio Crisp (11)
Queen Elizabeth's High School, Gainsborough

Cold

Coldness, that's the first and last thing I remembered, and by the look of the others around me, the same feeling was racing through their heads too: cold. It was only a matter of time before the end, we all knew it. I was waiting for someone to cut the silence, but no one did. I was about to break this deadlock when my captain did it for me. He whimpered, 'I'm going for a walk, I may be some time,' and he left the tent. Whatever happened I knew he suffered the same fate I will eventually suffer: cold.

Ewan Joseph (11)
Queen Elizabeth's High School, Gainsborough

Shattered Dreams

As the fear of crashing to the world below us became real, my heart sank. What was meant to be the happiest day of my life just possibly became the worst. Children were screaming for their mums and dads and that was when I realised I was never going to see my beloved family again. I didn't know what'd happened, my dreams had just shattered in front of me. My eyes filled with tears so my sight became blurry. I could hear ringing in my ears, my body became weak. It was all over, the end of my spectacular dream.

Lauren Ingram (14)
Queen Elizabeth's High School, Gainsborough

46

Wonderland's Finest Gone Wrong

I heard songs and laughter on the other side of the locked door that kept me safe. I once roamed that Wonderland without fear of anything, or anyone. Then everything changed... I caught a top hat which held a young girl on it, she was wanted, I helped her home and befriended her. We were best friends until she made me do horrible, evil, cruel, unspeakable things. The red queen was after me for the crimes I had committed. I was desperate, so I found someone who could keep me safe, but with a price. I took my mother's life.

Grace Russell (14)
Queen Elizabeth's High School, Gainsborough

Mysterious Hovercraft

I awake, seeing the bright lights of this land right before me. I look around only to see that I'm by myself stranded. Not knowing what to do I get up. But it's been trashed and there's no windows. Converted into a nervous wreck I approach a door. Slowly striding towards it I catch a handle. The door opens and flings me through it in a split second. I gain my self-consciousness back and pull myself back up only to be greeted by a monster who towers over me. Just here waiting for my certain death to begin straight away.

Nathan Dominic Gould (12)
Queen Elizabeth's High School, Gainsborough

The Man On The Moon

Years ago my spacecraft crashed on the moon. I'd lived on the moon ever since that day. Every night I sat on the edge of the moon fishing for golden meteorites to eat for supper, opposite Planet Earth. I liked to sit on my bench to observe the strange planet with my telescope which I'd kept.
I looked through the glass and saw a spaceship coming my way. I jumped up and waved. That caught his attention and he steered his vehicle to me and told me to hop in.
He pressed the button and we were off to Earth!

Oliwia Maria Brzozowska (12)
Queen Elizabeth's High School, Gainsborough

Possibility

My parents are selfish. Never have they ever looked at me, or even pointed in my direction. Their only goal is to sell me for money. Otherwise I'm no use to them.
Smoke covers the city like a thick blanket. Oil floods the grey suffocating streets. My parents ship oxygen from other places just to keep us living. We are people just like you, but money coats their brains, making them immune to the real world. Every morning I wake up and look at the petal beside me on the bedside table. It always gives me a flicker of hope.

Sadie Butler (13)
Queen Elizabeth's High School, Gainsborough

The American Dream?

Boom! As the planes collided into the building all I could see on my computer screen was flames. Of course I felt bad for this massacre, but I knew this would make everyone love me. No one could hate me for killing the man who supposedly masterminded this huge attack. All I had to do now was to wait as we pretended to look for him. Then pay him and his family to keep quiet. The few millions I'd be losing would be worth it as long as I was remembered as the greatest President in the history of America.

Ethan Rosslee (13)
Queen Elizabeth's High School, Gainsborough

Real Food

England, 2074. I was walking through the woods when I found a portal. I thought I would go in. I was off on a journey. I was sat at the table. My mum asked me what I wanted for tea. I stared. 'I would like pigs in blankets, fish fingers and chips.' I waited then it came. She gave me it. There was pigs in blankets, fish fingers, toads in holes. I sat down and closed my eyes. 'I wish I could go home.' Suddenly I appeared in front of plates of real food. Well I do love real food, yummy!

Lucy Dalton (11)
Queen Elizabeth's High School, Gainsborough

The Land Of Hearts

Imagine a world where everything was perfect. The love of your life fell in love with you at first sight. Well, in the land of hearts everything was like this.
A person would fall in love with you and never fall out of it. Everything in the land of hearts was vibrant red (to represent love). One example of a couple that lived in the land is Harry and Leah Mitchell. Everything in their life was perfect, all except their troubled son, Leonard. Nothing was more troubled than what he did in August 1985. It was to end the land.

Léonie Armstrong (11)
Queen Elizabeth's High School, Gainsborough

The End?

It was a fine day. At least until it struck! The explosion hit a few metres from my desk. It threw me out of my chair, then it hit again. The force of this threw me out of the seventy seventh window and I was falling fast.

Once I was outside everything went into slow motion and my whole life flashed before my eyes. My childhood, my birthdays, the odd detention and Christmases all led up to this moment. I was convinced this was where I would die. Suddenly at the fifth floor everything reverted to normal speed and then...

Oliver Phillips (11)
Queen Elizabeth's High School, Gainsborough

The Shallows

The depths of the ocean were nearing closer and closer as the seconds went by. The sense of fear for all passengers aboard could be smelt for miles on end. Screaming and cries for help, ringing in my ears, what do I do? Where do I go? Is this the end? With the water level slowly increasing and my heart pumping out of my chest with fear, I made a decision. *Splash!* The hard impact of my shaking body rippled the freezing cold water of the Pacific Ocean. With my body exhausted and drained, this was it, the final straw!

Elliot Simpson (13)

Queen Elizabeth's High School, Gainsborough

Betrayal

I walked out of my tent. The Beserkers had destroyed half our camp. I got my men into a wall of shields to repel attacks. I then saw the symbol of the Beserkers. They were from my ally up north... Had he betrayed me? Thirsty for more land? I had to put a stop to this new threat. I marched my army north to confront him. I put my troops in a double line formation. He had infantry superiority spread deep. I charged his Beserkers, my men clashing against his. I swung my cavalry around and killed all his men.

Jai Shivdev Nanthakumar (13)
Queen Elizabeth's High School, Gainsborough

The Rebel Of The Followers

All I have ever known is to follow him. It's what we all have to do. But it doesn't seem right to kill the innocent people. When we all go to our hard beds and the lights have been turned off, I whisper, 'Hey, do you think what we are doing is right?'

They all chorus, 'No!' then it hits me. We will rebel against he who has cared for us our whole lives. When we were babies, we were dumped, so he brought us up to know nothing but hunting and killing people. It seems wrong to kill him...

Poppy Hancock (13)
Queen Elizabeth's High School, Gainsborough

End Of Me

I awake, another day on this miserable planet they call Earth. It's been a year since the bombs dropped, wiping fifty-seven percent of the population out. I think they were the lucky ones! Ever since, the attacks haunt me in my dreams. I was there and I saw all the major powerhouses of the world. Buckingham Palace and the White House went down in the oblivion. After my family died in front of me, I mutated into a monster. This is it. This is the end of the planet. This is the end of everything. The end of me.

Sam Johnson (13)
Queen Elizabeth's High School, Gainsborough

Arch Enemies

There I was standing at the bottom of a pit, how I do not know, but I was petrified. The last thing I did was hit a guy in my house. That doesn't matter now because I heard a deep voice coming from the top of the pit with a shadow. 'Release the snakes!'

'OK.' As a trap door opened, hundreds of snakes fell on top of me. I screamed like mad. I was bit by a green snake. I could feel poison running up my leg. My veins turned red. Then I heard screams.

It was all a dream!

Mason Lewis Heslop (12)
Queen Elizabeth's High School, Gainsborough

A Change Of Events

I finished my maths test in ten minutes. I fell asleep.
When I woke up I was in a different room. The entire room
was in black and white and above the blackboard was a
picture in a frame of Adolf Hitler. My uniform was bland and
there was a shield on the pocket that said: 'Heil Hitler'.
Hitler had won the war. I stood up and ran out the room to
see Nazi flags over all the lockers. I sprinted to the nearest
one and smashed my head until I was unconscious. I woke
up in my geography lesson.

Cian Vaughan (12)
Queen Elizabeth's High School, Gainsborough

Water Disaster

As the water rose above my ankles, I could see the nervous looks on the faces around me. My knees started to tremble and my heart started to beat faster. The water was at my knees by this time and it was gradually getting higher. Suddenly, gushes of water splashed over my head, dragging me under, I struggled to get my head out of the water. I just needed one breath of the fresh air that was above the cold water that surrounded me. Finally I could stand up. The wave pool was as bad as I had originally thought.

Ben Ross (14)
Queen Elizabeth's High School, Gainsborough

Helping My Country

Darkness lay upon the soldiers of Iraq. Day after day they risk their lives while we sit here moaning about how we have not got the latest gadgets. My heart sinks and thumps in my stomach. I watch the advert on TV recruiting more soldiers, should I volunteer and leave my family to worry about me for the most of their lives? The flowery wallpaper in my room looks blurry, my head is spinning faster than a wheel on a Ferrari. I am going out to Iraq to help my country! Have I made the right decision? Will I survive?

Emma Jackson (12)
Queen Elizabeth's High School, Gainsborough

Land Of Hooves

I open my curtains and I feel the same sense of fascination towards this beautiful land as always. Today, is going to be a great day as Queen Urella, the unicorn, has provided the land with the most magnificent rainbow. This proves she is in a marvellous mood. As I hurry to work I bump into Herbie, he is my best friend, but is also the most mischievous donkey I have ever met! He tries to tempt me into going to breakfast instead of work. I hug him and tell him I will see him as soon as I finish.

Grace Sinclair (11)
Queen Elizabeth's High School, Gainsborough

A Day In The Life Of The Nix

I'm the Nix. A foul creature.

Today I got dressed, put my pants on my head and my shoes on my hands. I slimed myself up with lava and popped my eyes in. I got to work at eleven in the evening. I took out my eyes and put them in my hands. You could hear the screams in the room! I'm vile, disgusting, scary. When I finished work, I went home. My giant cockroach jumped up at me. I had only scared five thousand people tonight. Oh. I had a mud bath, brushed my armpits and went to bed. Peace.

Will John Daubney (12)
Queen Elizabeth's High School, Gainsborough

Through The Eyes Of My Horse

It's the final jump. I can see it, it's getting closer and closer, I know what to do. I can feel her nerves running straight down into me. But now, all of that has disappeared, she's getting into position. I am now waiting for my kick in the side, telling me to jump. But I know best. She kicked me a little late, but I was really in control. One, two, three, we've made it. She will be so proud of me, but now all I can think about is my extra large hay net waiting for me at home.

Lily Mettham (11)
Queen Elizabeth's High School, Gainsborough

A Change Of Scenery

I wake up and the world has changed... I see shiny cars roll down the road. I run out onto the pavement and the sunlight shines down on me. The buildings surround the city. As I walk closer to the beach, the air tastes of salt. I turn around and see pastel beach huts dotted along the coastline. The sea glistens as it gently laps against the sand. I walk back and pass a bakery and smell fresh pastries. The sky turns pink and the sun becomes a small disc in the sky. This is where I want to stay.

Hope Ward (12)
Queen Elizabeth's High School, Gainsborough

I'm Coming For You!

I put on my mask, grab the AK-47, I strap my vest on and enter the bank. As soon as I enter there is a panic, security charging at me, I throw flares in their direction and head for the huge vault. As I reach it the alarms go off, I have to act fast. I bring out an explosive charge and run for cover. As it explodes I'm knocked back and money flies everywhere. I get to my feet and charge into the vault. I look around and find the hostages that I'm saving. We all run away to safety.

James Welsh (13)
Queen Elizabeth's High School, Gainsborough

The Infinity Stones

'Eeeh! We've got to get to the command centre quick!
We've got to run!' *Puff, pant!* 'We're here. Good,
Christopher, you're here. There's trouble. Go to the
abandoned church and I'll fill you in on the way.'
'Gem, Julie, north. Jenny, Rocky - west. Me and Jean will
take the east. We will meet at the south.' Ten minutes later,
we arrived. 'Wait! There they are.'
'No! The Elecranors! Quick call a mystic Titan and Mini.'
Ha! Clang! Cling! Swoosh! They were defeated. The
seven stones of infinity, mind, power, will, rhythm, courage
and energy banished the monsters of evil!

Brandon Booth (11)
Somercotes Academy, Louth

9.1.2.

A golden, luxurious, world-wedging tower sank into the squelchy, absorbent, mucky squelch. The once sensational monument destroyed within one click.
Tallon was now in ruins. Tallon had been invaded by syncro monsters that had sought distinction on all.
The stone pillar of Karratet, the meeting place of the government. They gathered weekly to discuss the king.
Stood around the pillar they were punishingly pale, putridly shined monsters and a second party royally armoured, curbed winged men. It could only be assumed to be parliament and the syncro monsters working in alignment to wreak almost destructive havoc. *Bang! Boom!*

Daniel Straw (12)
Somercotes Academy, Louth

Struck 12 O'Clock

12 o'clock came. Roaring objects advanced from side to side, like they were playing a game of chess. Lights flickered rapidly. Historic tables stumbled looking like elderly men dancing. Victorian doors clashed like they were communicating with one another. The ground decomposed within a couple of minutes. Everything turned inside out. All the things around floated into the underworld. Rigid branches clashed into grizzled windows. Fractured pieces of houses split into half looking like the houses were ready to eat breakfast, lunch and dinner all in one. Seconds later everything had gone. Nothing was to be seen. Only darkness.

Chloe Taylor (12)
Somercotes Academy, Louth

Arcturus

Long ago in 1000BC, when disgraceful, gruesome people were around, some magical, rainbow-coloured unicorns came with their fluffy tails. They forced the people in Fiercesome Town to become their magic servants by zapping them with their sharp colourful horns that shoot lasers. After they made everyone servants they renamed the town Dexterity Land.

Three fabulous years later, the unicorns roamed Earth and renamed it Arcturus. To get from country to country, they used rainbows, so cars could cross, also they put on a competition on every month for a fascinating teleporter, so anyone could teleport to any country they liked.

George Thornton (11)
Somercotes Academy, Louth

The Rebellion

'Help!' shouted people.

'Mayday, mayday!' shouted the pilots. *Boom!*

Once upon a time there were two people called Neymar and Messi. These people were survivors of a plane crash. The plane crashed when they were going to a football match, Barcelona versus Valencia. Neymar and Messi knew that to be able to survive they would need money and food to survive. They had two hundred thousand Euros. They found what they wanted, a settlement. They bought everything they needed including a house. Then the evil clan of the Naavi came and strolled through, thinking they were the best ever.

Olly Edwards (12)

Somercotes Academy, Louth

Doomsday Land

Nobody expected it, but it happened. Cities wiped, towns obliterated. People disappeared. The nukes flew and that was how it started. Denzil the ex-Marine is fighting, and by his side is Felix his cat. They fight for whatever they have left. They're aiming for sanctuary, apparently it is a heaven energy food shelter. Many have tried to get there and many have died. Situated a hundred miles from America, in the myriad of death-defying lands, the creatures there could kill you in a blink or even kill you by blinking. If they survived they'd thrive and be victorious or perish.

Harry Betterridge (12)
Somercotes Academy, Louth

Colin The Carrot And Other Interesting Vegetables

Martin (code name Marrow) was at Colin the Carrot's parents' house, Mrs Swede and Pa-snip. They were having a heated discussion about Broc-ollie, Colin's older brother who had been working out in the field for the last six months. With the new regulations coming in it was getting a lot more dangerous. Tom-ato seemed to have his finger on the pulse although Aspara-gus seemed to have info from higher up the food chain. Unfortunately B-russel, who nobody liked, had been promoted, he was full of hot air. What a complete and butter disaster. The amazing vegetable police force was born.

William Howard
Somercotes Academy, Louth

Forever Alone

Smack! I don't know what happened. Everything was dark, Pitch-black. Nothing could have been more frightening than this. I could have been killed or even worse. Wait! Rewind. Please...

Flash! A sharp pain fluttered across my brain like nothing else mattered in the world. Suddenly, the sun started to rise and slap, the floor turned to smelly blood. Dead bodies would roam the earth forever. Everything would be taken over and there would be nothing left of us. Not even the sun. It would soon be taken over, never to be seen again. We would always be forever alone.

Charlotte Cooper (11)
Somercotes Academy, Louth

Bob And The Killer Gloons

Bob strolled out of his dwelling holding his trusty trowel and wearing his favourite flip-flops. To his left he noticed the severed limb of a Humplechock. Immediately he heard a rustling sound in his well kept gloony patch, little did he know it was a legion of killer Gloons. The leader was Colin Wimper, the meanest Gloon of all. Were the Gloons responsible for the Humplechock's death?

Day after day, Bob discovered dead Humplechocks littering the landscape, apart from on Moonday there was nothing. A silent gnawing began at his foot, the Gloons were attacking, poor old Bob perished!

Sam Greenwood (12)

Somercotes Academy, Louth

The Big Secret, The Big Mistake...

She placed her muddy trainer through the small door. A gust of warm wind brushed her messy brown hair off her shoulder. She gazed upon a magnificent city, engulfed in glowing flowers and inhabited by tiny yet beautiful fairies. They flew around happily. There were screams. They all looked at her. Then, huge monsters draped in moss burst through the city walls, stomping flowers, tearing buildings down, snatching fairies and throwing them into their mouths. She ran. She charged toward the exit, no turning back. She was being chased. She leapt through the door slamming it behind her. What happened?

Jennifer Atwell (11)
Somercotes Academy, Louth

Trouble In Fairydell

Down below in a magical world with magical
creatures a fairy ruled. Up above was the problem. Evil
trolls. Once before they destroyed everything. Soon again
as they wriggled through the only way into the magical world
and shattered, destroyed their homes, villages. They all
went into hiding whilst the princess escaped to the three
most magical good witches ever existing. They decided to
help. They made their way to troll centre. They went inside
and the fairy saw her villagers. One of them froze the trolls,
the other sent them flying into their fire while the last saved
everyone.

Isabel Wyer (12)
Somercotes Academy, Louth

Trickery

This story is a little different than the usual stories you hear. My best friend Adam and I were off to the train station, we noticed something unusual, there were little girls screaming, 'He is coming! He is coming!'
'Who?' we asked.
'The Dark Lord,' they shouted as if it was the most obvious thing in the world.
We turned around but nobody was there, but as we turned back around we saw all of the girls had disappeared. We were searching around and we turned back around to see dolls staring towards us and they screeched, 'We are coming!'

Kyle Sharp (13)
Somercotes Academy, Louth

Rules Are Made To Be Broken

Welcome to my world that was once a great civilisation, but one day every year, that one day no one can get over, the purge for twelve ruthless hours. For one night America becomes an uncivilised oblivion.

This is how my world ended. Midnight on the 5th July 2015. No one was safe: no rules, no laws and especially killing. This is when America's population decreases faster than you can blink.

When the population goes from 500,079 million to 400,079 million every year and people's friendships crumble like apple pie, that's how my world ends in a gloomy place.

Oliver Toothill (12)
Somercotes Academy, Louth

The Secret Ocean

The evolutionary blue ocean shimmered in excitement for the admirable summer party, which was soon to come. The mermaids' pink hair waved back and forth in the sea water. The plans were made, every single mermaid in the ocean kingdom was to attend. The mermaids wore their prettiest seashells and even the sea horses too. They all made their way deep down under and let their inner sparkle shine. However, all the deafening intimidating sharks came to dance as well and it wasn't charming. Lucky enough there were mermaids in need, they all wriggled their rainbow tails in the end.

Elisé-Anais Critchley (12)
Somercotes Academy, Louth

The Girl In The Closet

Blood drools hastily, oozing out the beaten wardrobe. The doors snap open leaving only her spine-chilling presence and her alarming figure. Her temptation overpowers me when I hear her possessing, deadly tune. I get drawn to it like a moth to a flame limbering closer and closer to a spider's web. There she lays venomously as her presence haunts me till my death despair. The room is level 98. Left alone, shaking under the thin bed sheet, I lay frozen as multiple thoughts clutter my mind. She is my best friend. Someone save me...

The girl in the closet.

Charlotte Merry (12)

Somercotes Academy, Louth

Why? Why Me?

Why? Why me? Please just reason with my victimless body!
If you don't give me a chance with them, then why do this?
Twentieth of December, what's new? Nothing! What's this?
Is it a nightmare world? The only active brain in this
household is the tenant, I hardly see him. My mother thinks
my black skin and eye is too ugly. If she thinks that then
why injure me?
'It's a fact you're a dunce!' screamed Mummy.
'Oh dear, naughty girl, just kill her already!' disclaimed the
ex-convict Bob.
Oh I do hate him, he should leave! Why? Why me?

Megan Louise Whetstone (13)
Somercotes Academy, Louth

Fantasy Island

Once upon a time there lived a unicorn called Crystal, she lived in Fantasy Island with other animals that were very different. When she went through the woods cantering, all of a sudden she stopped and heard a noise and saw a rabbit called Rainbow. 'Hello, do you want to be my friend?' she asked.

Crystal said, 'Yes.'

Then an evil witch came out of nowhere and started fighting with her powers and the battle continued, she was going to cast a spell to turn them into small ants. But her spell backfired and it turned her into an ant instead!

Chloe Motson (12)

Somercotes Academy, Louth

Northern Lights

Far, far away somewhere in Greenland a girl called Maya discovered the Northern Lights. They were beautiful and they shone down on the people of Greenland like watchful, guardian angels. However, a wicked dragon called Milo wanted to rule the kingdom. He sent balls of fire down to reign upon the people. Maya knew she had to defeat him. She entered into a quest to save Greenland and its people. She fought for many days. Her strength and determination eventually won over the dragon and she banished him to Hell for all eternity. The people crowned her magnificent Queen Maya!

Liljan Tindalid (11)
Somercotes Academy, Louth

London's Troubles

I went to sleep that night thinking, *what am I going to do in the holidays?* Then I fell straight to sleep. I woke up the next morning and my mum told me we were going to Harry Potter Studios.

When we got there Mum was looking for her sunglasses. Purely by accident I walked into a wall and uncovered a wonderland called London, where everything happens like David Cameron left Parliament. In the distance I saw a poster that said: 'Your mum is looking for you!' I saw her in the distance. But she was with someone else - who?

Katie Swallow (12)
Somercotes Academy, Louth

The Enchantress

That was it. Everyone was inside. It was sunset. Why, every day, at the same time does the happiness and the joy go, and everyone goes into their houses? LaTroy was determined to solve the mystery. On the fifteenth of May 2099, LaTroy snuck out of his ramshackle bunker and spied on everyone and everything. He gave up, but he noticed a quaint boy watching something. He was stood under an ancient oak tree which was a monster towering over him. Someone was there. It was the person you wouldn't expect to be out after dark. It was... The Enchantress.

Idena Short (11)
Somercotes Academy, Louth

The Abandoned Cottage!

Suddenly my eyes shot open with a massive gasp. The first thing I questioned was, 'Where am I?' I knew straight away that I wasn't in my bedroom. But I recognised the place that I was in, I was in the abandoned cottage in the woods. Remembering that last time my best friends were around, we saw the cottage. How did I get here? I hadn't been in the woods for at least two weeks. Then I heard Paige, Lily, Lola, Jake, Josh and my parents shouting my name. 'Mum, Dad, friends, I'm over here.' Then a spooky stranger came...

Claudia Senior (13)
Somercotes Academy, Louth

Skyrim

I run right into the battlefield. Dragons everywhere. I use my magic sword but they keep coming, then the grey beards start joining the fight, then over twenty people in the Elite guard come out. We then charge towards the more powerful dragons. The Elite guards are slashing. The grey beards shouting. Then He comes out! The elder dragon, Aldewin. I pull out Umbra the most powerful sword forged. In one hand sword, the other the magic. I run right at him, I stab his wings, immobilising him. I stab his tail off. I stab him in the neck. *Thump!*

Liam Wright (11)
Somercotes Academy, Louth

The Three Bangs

He heard three bangs coming from the toilet, each one louder than the other. *Blocked again,* he thought, as he lifted the toilet lid. Suddenly the hand shot towards his throat. As it gripped tighter the pus-filled boils on the arm burst and purulent yellowy green discharge ran down its sinuous decomposing satanic flesh. He screamed, shouted, hoped and prayed, but he knew this was the end. He was being pulled towards the water...

His eyes opened, bloodshot, he was in bed. Just a dream... Then he heard three bangs, each one louder than the other.

Emily Ackroyd (12)
Somercotes Academy, Louth

Darkness...

As I entered the bizarre room I saw something that looked familiar. A fairy! It had diamond wings crested with jewels. Her eyes glinted at me as if she had been paralysed! I shuffled over to her, she didn't move. She was ice cold! I turned away from the fairy as I heard a crash from the kitchen. I jumped off the chair. Trembling from the presence of this creature of some sort, I walked slowly and crept to the kitchen. The knives were gone! My heart pounded in my chest. A figure appeared behind me, screeching loudly. I fell.

Onyx Clancy (11)
Somercotes Academy, Louth

Malpie Warzone

In the world of Malpie Warzone, the creatures were deep in war. Milltroy, one of the strongest creatures on the planet, was raging as a battle had destroyed his house. He was terrorising the little ones. His three fists were smashing everyone but the top three creatures hadn't come yet. The bullying had smashed and crashed all of the nearby houses. Usually when fights break out the strongest and feared monsters come break it up. But this was going to be hard. His team showed up. Five of the top monsters were attacking. The top three came to save them.

Reece Cook (11)
Somercotes Academy, Louth

The End Of Galactic Activity!

Bang! Bullets of magic flew from the walls. Children were screaming and running everywhere. We had to escape. There was nowhere else to go. What should I do? 'I'm so confused! Help!' I screamed.

My mother, father and brothers both got trapped and taken into the other world. We don't talk about the other world. It is a place that we forget because all of the horrible things that have happened there. Let's just say that we are doomed. If they have taken a few of us, we are all going to die. This is the very end!

Manisha Bains (13)
Somercotes Academy, Louth

Wings

I have wings! It's not a dream! I'm running... Well flying for my life with my diminutive flock behind me. We are reverberating, trying to escape from these satanic demons. They are tracking us down; they are following us everywhere we go. My friends and I are constantly being tortured. We are now soaring through the streets of New York trying to scavenge some food, trying to find somewhere to stay. We are abandoned avian hybrids and this is how we live...

Exposed to the harsh reality of human nature. Enduring it is the only option we have!

Hope Midgley (13)

Somercotes Academy, Louth

The Fog Demon

It was the morning of the new moon. The day of destruction.
No one could have foreseen this tragedy. Fenolda, the
daughter of chief of the Saplings, was exploring the
unexplored territories. She gazed at the sapphire blue sky,
the lush trees swaying to the wind's lullaby. She was
awoken from her trance-like state by an ear-piercing
scream. It was one of her enemies, a member of the
Phoenix Tribe. Suddenly, a wave of fog came crashing over
the trees. A towering demon formed from the fog. It sucked
the life out of Fenolda's enemy. The fog vanished...

Isobel Russell (12)
Somercotes Academy, Louth

The End

It was a peaceful world until... *Bang!* Bombs drop from the sky. It is horrible.

Scared, I start to fire my powerful gun. The rocky ground breaks as I climb up the hill. A bullet barely misses my head as I peer my eyes over the grass. I glance over my shoulder to see brave team-mates fighting ferociously. Their eyes are full of fear, but they are determined nobody is giving up. The rain is getting stronger, but this makes us stronger and stronger. Suddenly out of nowhere a bullet fires towards my face, but it is too late... Gone...

Evie Dinah Ann Kidd (12)
Somercotes Academy, Louth

Yasmine's True Story

Yasmine had one older brother and a younger brother and a sister. Her parents loved each other so much.

However, their life was soon going to destroy them all.

When Yasmine was four, her parents got the news that their little girl was dying of a brain tumour.

They were not sure how long they had left with her, but they didn't care, they did everything to make sure she had a proper send off.

Unfortunately Yasmine died when she was five. Her mum wasn't letting God take the others away too. Their lives had completely been destroyed.

Lydia Wright (13)
Somercotes Academy, Louth

Unbelievable Eland

There they were. Marching towards me as if they were butter spreading across some toast. My heart was pounding and my brain was telling me, 'This is the end.' Its fire breath beamed down on the town, killing everything in its path. I grabbed my sword and charged. It was getting dark, the clouds were candyfloss and the sun had fallen. But it was too late, the town was ashes, they had won. I wandered into the mountains to live there.
There was a strange wizard that whispered slowly into my ear and said, 'You come in.' So, I did!

Ella Pickard (11)
Somercotes Academy, Louth

Love Fantasy

My heart trembled as he approached with a twinkle in his bright eyes. He asked me to the prom. My heart skipped as he smiled. I crumbled under pressure and said, 'Um, yum.' He looked at me with a confused look. I was happy with my crush as my date. 'My life's complete,' I shouted. I was lucky that nobody heard me.

Then came the prom. I got scared, but he pulled up in his car, got out and leant in for a kiss! Suddenly I woke up, shaking but excited to see if he'd ask me in real life.

Isabell Harris (13)
Somercotes Academy, Louth

The Ghost Rider

The haunted horse came trotting towards the village, the rider's body was wrapped in a deep red cloak, pulled up so it formed a hood over his head. Suddenly its abdomen began pulsating. Something was fighting to get out. All of a sudden his mouldy skin fell off revealing devil wings, which allowed him to shoot up into the air! We huddled together, terrified, as it seemingly rode out of view! Thinking we were safe, shards of glass came raining down, slashing us! We ran for cover, the phantom appeared in the moonlight. This time he was not alone...

Aaron Steer (12)
Somercotes Academy, Louth

Cuteness Is Not Everything

There is a magical place called Sweetopia. It was underneath Jemima's bed. Every so often, she would go into this magical place.

One day, she went down into this magical place, she met the citizens, they were very artistic and social. One day, a new citizen came, he had long black hair, perfect blue eyes and the perfect white smile. They fell in love.

Suddenly, he started to act strange, he ignored her, paid no attention to her and he started to eat the citizens. So he was frozen for eternity only for someone to come and save him.

Thea Hussey (11)
Somercotes Academy, Louth

The Mysterious Creature!

I was walking along the wet, long pathway as the sun was slowly setting and the sky was flossy pink. The long chestnut brown trees were appearing over the sun as the light beamed in my face like a baby who has just opened its eyes for the first time. I felt shaking on my back, I then heard a mysterious sound in the smoky sky. The moon appeared black. I heard something in the distance. A massive animal appeared. The creature looked like a dragon with red scales. I ran, the floor cracked. I ran as fast as possible.

Jessica Butterfield (12)
Somercotes Academy, Louth

Rebellion Earth

We ran as fast as lightning because of Ellie. She and Courtney began to run fast because she'd seen the black dull dangerous guns in our deep pockets. They were trapped in the dark little corner at the side of the wall. Courtney went for Kacey so I got the black solid gun out of my deep pocket. *Bang! Bang!* Blood was dripping everywhere like red wine pouring out the bottle. We could hear the sirens coming, we all jumped rapidly over the wall. We were running as fast and quickly as possible, but the police caught up with us.

Leah Hezzell
Somercotes Academy, Louth

Cloud Town

Up, up was a cloud town where there was a special dust fairy called Magic. She was special because Magic did not have any friends or any parents. But Magic was special because she went on a dangerous adventure to fight the most miserable dust fairy in dust town. She went on an adventure where she had to swim through a crocodile pond and jump through fire hoops and last of all fight dust ninjas and the dark dust fairy. This fight went incredibly well and of course she won. All good people win. She's different. This changed her life.

Ellie Rusling (12)
Somercotes Academy, Louth

Once Upon A Storybook Lane

(Inspired by 'Once Upon A Time')

Once upon a stormy night a princess called Snow White had a daughter called Emma Swan. The queen wanted to kill this baby of Snows. The queen was racing down to Snow's castle and she was nearly there. Three moments later she arrived. She slammed her carriage door shut and stormed into the room and demanded the baby.
While this was happening the prince was fighting the evil queen's men, but the prince won with the baby in his arms. He then put the baby in a cupboard for safety so the queen wouldn't find her.

Billie Jay Wilson (13)
Somercotes Academy, Louth

23 Days...

My neck rubbed against the car, rust sprinkled onto my bloody T-shirt. I stood up, looking around in case they saw me. I grabbed my rucksack. I had to find food, I was starving. Bodies flooded the city. I stumbled across a warehouse, I kicked open the door. The warehouse seemed empty, I couldn't take any chances. I pulled out my knife. A blood trail led to a door. I crept up. A flesh-eating zombie knocked me over, grabbing my neck. I kicked out and ran. It caught me. I stabbed it to death. I was alone, infected and dying...

Eliot James Coleman (11)
Somercotes Academy, Louth

The Devil's Angel

Imagine a world split in half: half good, half evil. Black and desolate. Harry was born into this world, giving him magical powers. As Harry grew, he ventured from his cave. In the distance, war was raging. Harry realised the war was over him. Whilst hunting, he saw a dragon. He sprinted towards the dragon, all he wanted was for the fighting to stop. Harry planned to ask the dragon to kill half the world, but which side should he choose? The dragon soared through the air, intent on ending the war. He had made his decision, but had Harry?

Charlotte Wright (11)
Somercotes Academy, Louth

Troll Princess

One day the Queen and King had a baby princess troll. Her name was Teagan, she was born on a bad day because the ogres came and ruined their land. However, the king saved everyone saying no trolls to be left behind. So everyone managed to go away from them.

Five years passed... Princess Teagan and her family had the kingdom and there was one troll called Alex who was miserable because of all the ogres, but when he met Princess Teagan he was happier than ever, since then he had cuddle time. The ogres never came back ever again.

Lucy-Leigh Killick
Somercotes Academy, Louth

The Knight's Realm

In a world far away from here, there was a king who was showered in jewellery and only the finest clothing and he had a lovely daughter. The king trusted two of his best knights. one with shining and clean armour and the other with dark coal-like armour.

One day the king was attacked by a Treger-Snipe. A small beast but deadly, it poisoned the king. He grew weak and shortly passed away, but before he passed away, he gave his crown to the black knight and his daughter's hand in marriage and they took their wedding vows.

Oscar Wilson (11)
Somercotes Academy, Louth

The Morning Of The Big Day!

My hand clutched onto the bedroom door of my son's room. But he wasn't there! Where was he? It was the day when my son was going to his father's wedding and he wasn't even home. I strolled into his room slowly. *Bang!* went the door once I had opened it. The door creaked very slowly when I started to close it. *Crash! Bang! Smash!* The crystal door handle fell off. The curtains were flying everywhere as the window was open and then I started to see a hand coming through the window. It creaked!

Skie Jasmine Shelton (12)
Somercotes Academy, Louth

The Mysterious World

I opened the mysterious door and went inside. I was astounded, my jaw dropped. It was ever so sunny, there were rainbows, rabbits, butterflies and all cute and fluffy things. There were marshmallow houses and everybody was so nice. I looked down from where I was and saw where I used to live. Everybody was fighting, it was raining and stormy. I was sad and my heart disappeared. I had to go back there. I was so happy here but I had to go back. Soon I opened the door and appeared in my boring old and dusty bedroom.

Charlie Beevers (12)
Somercotes Academy, Louth

The Dinkster's Search For His Clothes

The Dinkster had awoken in a bundle of mess and shot up needing something to wear, yet no clothes were in sight. So he searched around his house looking under his sofa and in his closet, yet still nothing to be found. Then he suddenly remembered he threw his clothing into the tumble dryer so he darted to his tumble dryer and laid all his clothing to the side knowing he now had to choose what he'd wear. After searching through the pile of clothes he had for twenty minutes, he found some clothing he was happy with wearing.

Leo Burch (12)

Somercotes Academy, Louth

Far Away

One dark and stormy night, the sky was grey and misty. All you could see was a shadow of the gloomy distance. Midnight struck, the clocks turned back an hour. All the shops were shut. Suddenly there was a loud noise, *bang, bang, bang.* It was coming from the front door. I contemplated should I stay or should I go? Laid there was a sealed envelope. Inside was a golden key and a letter from my long-lost dad. He was trapped in another realm, I had to see him! I was so eager to see him, I was so desperate.

Grace Power (11)
Somercotes Academy, Louth

Planet Zundar

From an unreal view, the Planet Zundar looked like a purple Earth, as each leg was of a deep violet and the creatures that lurked the depths of the sweetly coloured forest. From big to small each animal had a way of surviving, for example the raptor deer as it accelerated to eighty-five miles per hour, it could outrun anything, except a stray arrow shot by the most intelligent hunter on the Planet, Ishback. Translated to English, it means warrior and he was a great one at that. Well, until he was hunted by wretched, horrid humans.

Travis Broughton (11)
Somercotes Academy, Louth

Terror Of The Dragon

I was in the rotted theme park. Forced to stay there due to my inquisitive nature, I prepared to explore the park. I felt nervous. Cautiously I crept around looking at the broken rides. One looked like a thriller. It had a lot of loops. Suddenly a magical man appeared, he came up to me and said, 'Do you want me to turn this park to life again?' I said, 'Of course!' Before my eyes the theme park was brought to life. I looked up to the sky. A huge dragon with wings as big as an aeroplane swooped down!

James Garcia-Fussey (12)
Somercotes Academy, Louth

Dragontopia

It was a normal day at the normal time of 8:45. Jack and I were walking to Block Square. We were going to work, but suddenly the ground started to shake! Out of nowhere this bloodshot, flame fire breathing dragon came down from the sky, burning buildings down, setting things on fire. For all we knew this was the end. Jack fell to the cracked floor. And soon after so did I. The dragon had taken us down. My eyes slowly started to open. Heaven? I looked next to me. Jack wasn't there anymore. I saw the Ramshackle City.

Teanna Willey (11)
Somercotes Academy, Louth

What's Inside?

Belle's hand vibrated. Her whole body became a stiff statue as she struggled to make it to the rusty door. The mail flung out of her hand, she charged after it, just managing to grab on to it. The broken door squeaked as she glanced inside. *Tick-tock.* As she put one foot in front of the other, a sweaty dry sickening smell came clobbering in and struck her hard in the face. She made her way up the disintegrating stairs, then pushed her feet into the right hand side room, then gazed upon a nightmare mess of a body...

Rebecca Jeffrey (12)
Somercotes Academy, Louth

Pink Problem

I looked at the grand portal in front of me. I looked back at my friends and let out a sigh; I didn't want to go. I stepped through the portal and was in a place. 'I don't understand,' I said to myself. The whole place was pink!

I hate the colour pink! Maybe it was an upside down place. I wandered around until I had to go. The pink was getting to me. When I came back through the huge portal, I was back at home, my friends and family came and hugged me!

That was my fantasy adventure!

Maisie Thomas (12)

Somercotes Academy, Louth

Rogue

I wake up feeling hazy and sick. I step onto the cobbled concrete. The water runs through the cranny's creaking mini rivers. I grab the soggy telegraph and head back inside. It says about a murder. I realise that if I can solve this maybe I can regain my job. I grab my forty-four calibre pistol and swing open the door onto the dimly lit street once again. I make my way through the congregation of houses, the rain runs off my coat forming small roads. I spin and aim my gun, I shoot, I see the body. I'm Rogue!

Benjamin Thomas Jackson (12)

Somercotes Academy, Louth

The Gobble-Pop Sanctuary

As the rain stormed down on the road, I walked up to the park. Before I could get there I heard a noise, not a normal noise you hear in Candy-iniza with chocolate as grass. Oh! I'm Candice. As you can tell I'm a gummy bear. That noise was coming from the Candy-drops. I went over to the noise and I saw a Gobble-pop. A Gobble-pop is a terrifying monster that you don't see here. It grabbed me. I stumbled back and fell on the chocolate covered road. My head hit the path and it took me to the Gobble-pop sanctuary.

Daisy Tellefsen (11)

Somercotes Academy, Louth

The White Winter Wonderland

I walked into a White Winter Wonderland; it was a magical place. There was an emerald tunnel before me, I walked through. It felt ice cold.

A devil appeared. I was frightened, and scared, there was no way out...

The devil cast a spell to make the tunnel contract. The only way out was to get the key. The key was hidden under the ground. I had to dig quickly, as the tunnel was becoming shorter and shorter, soon I would be squashed. Just in time I found it. Hurriedly I turned the key in the lock. A path appeared.

Harriet Gilliatt (11)
Somercotes Academy, Louth

Escaping From The Past

It was wet and humid, how could I escape? Juice of the sweat from the slaves above fell on my head. I felt mortified. My abusive masters came in and demanded we had to go to sleep as we had to be up in two hours. This was my moment to finally make the great escape. I crawled through the miniscule gap in the archaic wall. Clambering through the dusty floor, I saw sunlight. My face had the happiest grin. But from the corner of my eye I saw my masters chasing me. How would I escape?

Freya Elise Donner (13)

Somercotes Academy, Louth

Untitled

'Grab your guns and head to the alley now!' I screamed. Kenny was racing there with his son Duck, Katjaa and Clementine. I pulled down a shelf to slow them down.
Five days later we were in the Motor Inn. Glen had left and we were just scared by the people at the dairy! But now Clementine was kicking the ball, Duck was bitten and Kenny was stressed out. I tried to calm everyone down, but it didn't work. In the corner of my eye I saw a horde coming this way and told everyone to go! But I failed.

Ryan Tomlinson (11)
Somercotes Academy, Louth

The Eleven Rings

In a place far away from here, eleven rings were created. Four of them were warrior guards. Five of them were guards. The other two were a king and a president. They ruled Birk.

Birk was a very huge island. They ruled well, but the king got poisoned by a witch. She ruled the land badly and killed children and women. The ten rings retreated when the king died, so they all went to a battle. The witch resisted and killed nine of them. But one killed the witch. The king was now back and he ruled forever.

Kristian Sivertsen (12)

Somercotes Academy, Louth

How I Came To This Realm

Peter lived in a decent village. He had blonde hair that swayed in the wind. His village had emerald green grass, the air was pure as a diamond. Peter was playing with his friend Carl. He dared Peter to jump through the tyre on an old, run-down tree. Just as Peter started to jump a vortex opened up in front of the tyre. All of a sudden a chill ran down Peter's spine. He thought to himself, *oh my God.* As he jumped through the vortex he was stunned at what he saw. A beautiful realm stood before him.

Leo Jacob Whittaker (11)
Somercotes Academy, Louth

Monster Land

Once upon a time there was a little boy who set a trap for the monster that came into his bedroom every night. It was a line, but it didn't work as he found out in time. Although the monster was a bit dumb, he forgave the boy and asked him for his help. The boy agreed and they went to Monster Land. The boy was wearing a light suit as light was their weakness. So when they got to the leader's lair the boy turned his lights on. The monster blew up but rebuilt itself and killed the boy.

George Crawford (12)

Somercotes Academy, Louth

Z-Land

Tom heard moaning from the basement, and he knew the zombies would be hungry for brains. He opened the door and ran for it. He ran and ran for his life. He picked up a crowbar and hit the zombie on his head. He saw a clear path to safety. He ran for his life, but he got hit and he fell to the ground. He woke up and his eyesight was terrible. He focused again and he saw zombies coming after him and he knew he was gone. He said his last words and prepared for death: 'Bye.'

Jake Mudie (13)
Somercotes Academy, Louth

Into The Darkness

As I wandered into the old, gloomy cave I heard a voice beckoning me in.
Nobody was there. I took a few more steps inside and something ran behind me. Again there was no one there. A fire lit at the end of a long, winding tunnel. Still no one there. I didn't know where I was or if I was going to return home again. An old, hunched over woman watched me and every move I made. The door slammed shut behind me and I was trapped. She came towards me walking then running! That's all I remember.

Hollie-Mae Smith (12)

Somercotes Academy, Louth

Gravesland

It was a gloomy night. Fog filled the atmosphere. It seemed like a different world. Fair enough it was in an ancient graveyard. I was determined to do it. I was determined to see a dead body. All of a sudden the world went cold, it sent a shiver down my spine. Then a tap on my shoulder. I turned around to face a hideous creature. I tried to run. It was no good. It had got me. I made the loudest ear piercing scream, hoping someone heard me. A cold hand was smacked over my mouth. Will I survive?

Amy Baxter-Rowson (11)
Somercotes Academy, Louth

Untitled

As I walked through the gap in the wall of my house, I realised that it wasn't part of my house, it was a new world. In the distance there was a burst of fire and a loud roar. All of a sudden a giant winged beast flew over me and headed towards the castle behind me. It fell out the sky in front of me. I started to head to the castle. At the gates they weren't human, they were half bull, half human. They raised their spears and pointed them at me and charged at me like bulls!

Jack Row (11)
Somercotes Academy, Louth

The South Park

Once upon a time there was a lovely forest that people could visit to see the outstanding view of the enormous sea and amazing cliffs. But a group of boys came not to just see the cliffs, but to jump off them into the sea. That meant the poor old man who owned it got taken down because it was too dangerous. The man was furious with them and started taking his anger out on the forest. He chopped all the trees down and set them on fire. But then he was cursed and went mad for life.

Frazer Perrow (11)
Somercotes Academy, Louth

The Bridge

On the bridge standing right in front of me was the man I saw from the other day. He threatened me. He gave me a look to say, 'Get out of my way.' But what if I didn't, what could he do about it?

Then all of a sudden a bright light shone above me, I plucked it out of the air and threw it to the ground. The second it landed a magical black hole appeared, he fell like a bird from the sky. I saw it in slow motion. It was brilliant, he'd gone now. Nice and peaceful.

Joe Bradley Jordan (11)
Somercotes Academy, Louth

Untitled

One day it was so cold on Snowland. No one went out their house. There were four people that died because they went out. Someone made it to the cave and they were still in it and no one had seen him since. I went down there and there were loads of dead bodies. They were rotten and some had just been killed. There was no sign of the person that survived when it was cold. I ran out and ran back to my house and locked up. I went to sleep and no one ever went there again!

Oliver Greenway (11)
Somercotes Academy, Louth

The Boss

In England, a man named Derek Nicholls is a businessman in London. He is a rich man, but involved with the mob, in fact he is the boss. He has two wives. His son drove to an old river with a rival leader in his boot, he then shot him and Derek dumped him in the river. Now Derek is the big boss. So they then massacred the government in Westminster, it was a bloodbath. He now sits at the head of the table drinking port, now owning London. The next on his list is the world!

Tarn Nicholls (12)

Somercotes Academy, Louth

New World

I saw a figure in the distance. Tall and threatening. It didn't move, it just stood there. Looking at me. I couldn't see in his eyes, but he had a long tongue that was swirling around. I froze for a second and looked for a way out. I saw a way to get to my loop so I could get home. Max was there with a gun. I got eye contact with him and he took the last shot right in the face! The rest of them came, we were safe again, and we were going home at last.

Alysia Lloyd-Clews (12)
Somercotes Academy, Louth

Mission To Hell

Devilyn looked in a mirror and saw ugliness. Devilyn was a girl who was bullied and was a waste of space some people said. Twins Hannah and Monty were larking around as usual. But Hannah wanted to reunite with Devilyn.
Ping! went Devilyn's phone: 'Hi Devilyn, want to meet up?' In a furious rage Devilyn was tempted to throw her phone on the floor.
Three weeks later they met up and Devilyn was really mean to Hannah.
'But why are you being so mean?' Hannah asked.
'My plan's to get rid of you because you said I'm ugly!'
'No!'

Ruby Grace Allen (11)
Spalding Academy, Spalding

Winter

'Hello, somebody there? Hello? No it's all white everywhere. Is somebody here? Well I guess no one is here... But I can see footprints, I think that it is from an animal. I wonder where they take me?'
'Miaow! Miaow!'
'It's a cat? Where is it coming from?'
For a moment it all went black. 'What is going on?'
'Miaow! Miaow!' It was snowing, but from where? There was no sky, no clouds, weird. Snow! Snow! Everywhere!
'Maybe it's not a cat, it is a girl singing, why is she singing like a cat? Maybe she is a witch?'

Georgiana Comanescu (13)
Spalding Academy, Spalding

The Rich Wonderland

There was a girl called Grace who was thirteen years old, she had an older sister who wasn't nice, she hated Grace. She had a stepmother and dad.

They lived in a small, poor house, although they could get a huge house for only two hundred pounds, they didn't get the house. Grace also had a nice grandma, she lived in a dream house. Grace hated living with her stepmother and dad because they were rude to Grace and they didn't give much love and support needed. So Grace had enough, so she ran away to her nice sweet grandma.

Ketia Ela Lace (13)
Spalding Academy, Spalding

138

Planet Of Wonder

On a planet far away three million people said the planet was called Planet of Wonder. It was a futuristic planet of 2020. The land was very flat, four cities were all going well until the planet was attacked by big green disgusting aliens. All the cities got terrorised, all the schools were destroyed. Luckily someone came out of the dark black sky to save our planet. He helped loads of people from buildings and rubble. He got all the aliens off the planet. Everyone was saved from the aliens by a mysterious man. No one knew where he came from.

Brayden Hagon (12)
Spalding Academy, Spalding

The Vamps Wonderland

Welcome to this amazing, wonderful world of Vamps in Birmingham. It's open from 10am - 1am. It's a place with lots to do. See the Vamps perform live for free. Go see their dressing room and go on a Vamps roller coaster. The Vamps and I live in the wonderland. Created by the Vamps for their fans.

A young girl came to the Vamps Land and went on the roller coaster and it got stuck and started to rock side to side. The girl was screaming. Connor from the Vamps came running to help. He climbed to the top to save her.

Deborah Batch (14)
Spalding Academy, Spalding

The Candy World

One day my friends and I were walking towards the deserted forest. This was our special hiding place. It had a secret. Inside our forest was a wooden door hidden in a big oak tree. Inside the tree was our secret stash of candy. Nobody could enter this tree, only us, as we had the special key. This was our candy wonderland where we could feast ourselves on all of the good treats that were inside the tree. But one day we all went to the tree and something strange had happened; the wooden door was wide open.

Emma Clark (13)
Spalding Academy, Spalding

True Love Is Pain

Once upon a time, a princess named Brooklyn was in love with a villager named James. It was true love, but Brooklyn was being forced to marry a prince named Gale! Every night, Brooklyn and James snuck out and met up.
One night, James prepared a picnic and it was very romantic! Brooklyn was surprised by this gesture and suddenly James proposed to her! She said yes and ran off home to tell her family. Her mother was happy, but her father was furious! He took her to the roof space and executed her. Then James killed himself...

Erin Langford (11)
Spalding Academy, Spalding

A Magical Conundrum

Coco had coal-black hair and wicked sea-green eyes. One day, Coco visited the zoo to see the lions. Unfortunately for Coco she accidentally uses her magic to free the lions. Coco ran to her house to find the book of spells. 'The spell is Flyoara Migora.' Coco sprinted like a greyhound towards the zoo, only to find the lions on a rampage! Coco got her spell book out and said, 'Flyoara Migora,' The lions went back to their cages, and Coco was in the newspaper for saving the day!

Hannah Dawson (14)
Spalding Academy, Spalding

Welcome To Wonderland

It was England 2014, Chelsea had just won the FA Cup, it was the best day of our lives. Suddenly there was turbulence. The captain said, 'Hang on!'
Suddenly, it went black, no one was there. Then there was light and we could see again. The Captain said, 'We're going to land.' We landed. It was hot and cold, it was dreadful. No one was there. We were on a beach, but it was different. There was a parcel so we opened it quickly and it contained next year's paper. Our team no longer existed.

Connor Young (14)
Spalding Academy, Spalding

Kingsley And Ben

Once upon a time there was a boy called Ben. He was in Year 6 and he was a nice boy but there was one thing about him, he got bullied every day and when it was lunchtime the people he called friends stole his money. He was so scared to start secondary school until Kingsley started at his school. He got bullied as well. Every day Ben saw him get bullied until they started secondary school. They were best friends and the best thing was they did not get bullied and they got huge grades and a best friend.

Millie Bailey (11)
Spalding Academy, Spalding

Son's Birthday

Once on Earth, there was a man named Andrew. He lived in London. He had a family, a wife and two sons. He was an astronaut and he explored Mars.

June 21st, he had to, would go to Mars, but it was his son's birthday. He wanted his father to remain on Earth for his birthday. But his father had told his son that if he delayed the flight there would be lots of problems with landing on Mars. So he had to go today. Andrew was told that he would be able to celebrate the birthday on the Internet.

Jantraskin Jan (14)

Spalding Academy, Spalding

The Death Dream Land

There was a person called Joe and he was being chased by the police, but he got caught by the police. He was put in jail for a murder. The police decided to put Joe in a world for prisoners that were staying in jail for the rest of their lives. When he got there he was pleased and thought it was good. Eventually he got rich and lived a happy life until more prisoners came. It turned his life around, the other prisoners became rich, but after a while they got bored and started searching for a way out.

Tyler James Boon (11)
Spalding Academy, Spalding

My World

My world is called Earth. On Earth we are in the future 2100. My world is really nice because people are working for money and they never steal. The landscape is very beautiful because on our planet we have mountains and a big seaside. On the Earth are many living people, children, old people and animals. The weather is nice because it is warm and you can go to the beach. My world was made by God, and he made two people, a man and a woman and through them the world was made to be by honest people.

Maria Chirita (11)

Spalding Academy, Spalding

Graceland

There was once a world called Graceland. It was the one place everyone wanted to visit. It was always hot and everyone was always happy. The best part of Graceland was that everything was free. Everything was run by automatic robots who acted as human.
One day the robots turned and started to eat the humans. There was nothing that the humans could do except to set the robots on fire. The problem was that everything else was getting set on fire. This caused a wire to catch light and the world blew up.

Grace Woods (15)
Spalding Academy, Spalding

Percy And Wally's Adventures

Percy Penguin and Wally Walrus are chilling on the edge of the ice and are about to go for a swim. As they're about to hop in, the ice splits and Wally floats away. The ice hits another part of the island. Wally then sets off on his journey home. Meanwhile, Percy sets off on his journey to find Wally.

One day later Percy sees Wally lying on a bit of floating ice, so he jumps in, finds some fish and takes them to Wally. Percy takes Wally home and they celebrate Christmas together again!

Caitlin Langford (14)

Spalding Academy, Spalding

Waterproof England

It's England 2080. There are no plants and no trees. The whole of England is just grey with no colour. It's all dark and wet. The people live in floating waterproof houses. They still have computers and phones and look after their pets. When people want to go to the shop they have to go on a waterproof car and drive there. When God died due to all the stress of the world the angels cried and wouldn't stop. People had to deal with all the water. It was a very sad place to live.

Amy Clark (13)
Spalding Academy, Spalding

Jack And The Rocket Ship

Once upon a time there was a boy named Jack and he really liked rocket ships. His dream job was to be an astronaut so that he could fly a rocket ship and he would have a chance to go to the moon. He had an older brother aged fifteen who said he would never make it, but he was determined to prove him wrong. So he really started to knuckle down and get good grades at school. He knew he had to train lots to be an astronaut, and to be able for him to drive a rocket ship.

Thomas Maddison (12)

Spalding Academy, Spalding

The Holiday

Once upon a time there was a boy named Charlie, he was a boy who felt sorry for his family because they were poor.
They were planning on going to the Big Apple, which is known as the one and only New York.
They had to go on three planes and one bus, then they would be at the hotel.
When they got there, they put all the stuff away in the hotel and then had a look around. They also go went for tea.
Then they went and looked around New York and took pictures.

Liam Crane (13)
Spalding Academy, Spalding

Magic Rabbits

One day a man put an egg on his mat and he left the country that night.
When he arrived home there was a large rabbit sitting where the egg was, it was a fluffy rabbit. He kept the rabbit and it had lots of rabbits, some were big and some were small. Some could even talk. They had ten girls and ten boys, so the man decided to sell the rabbits and he decided to keep one for himself.
His was the only place you could buy a rabbit.

Emma Rose Pates
Spalding Academy, Spalding

Young**Writers**
Est.1991

YOUNG WRITERS INFORMATION

We hope you have enjoyed reading this book – and that you will continue to in the coming years.

If you're a young writer who enjoys reading and creative writing, or the parent of an enthusiastic poet or story writer, do visit our website **www.youngwriters.co.uk**. Here you will find free competitions, workshops and games, as well as recommended reads, a poetry glossary and our blog.

If you would like to order further copies of this book, or any of our other titles, then please give us a call or visit **www.youngwriters.co.uk**.

Young Writers
Remus House
Coltsfoot Drive
Peterborough
PE2 9BF
(01733) 890066
info@youngwriters.co.uk